Dealing with Your Feelings

Sometimes We Feel Jealous

By Leona Fowler

Cavendish Square
New York

Published in 2022 by Cavendish Square Publishing, LLC
243 5th Avenue, Suite 136, New York, NY 10016

First Edition

Library of Congress Cataloging-in-Publication Data

Names: Fowler, Leona, author.
Title: Sometimes we feel jealous / Leona Fowler.
Description: New York : Cavendish Square Publishing, [2022] | Series:
Dealing with your feelings | Includes index.
Identifiers: LCCN 2020030634 | ISBN 9781502660008 (library binding) | ISBN
9781502659989 (paperback) | ISBN 9781502659996 (set) | ISBN
9781502660015 (ebook)
Subjects: LCSH: Jealousy in children–Juvenile literature. |
Jealousy–Juvenile literature.
Classification: LCC BF723.J4 B44 2022 | DDC 155.4/1248–dc23
LC record available at https://lccn.loc.gov/2020030634

Editor: Caitie McAneney
Designer: Deanna Paternostro

The photographs in this book are used by permission and through the courtesy of: Cover Prostock-studio/Shutterstock.com; p. 5 JackF/iStock/Getty Images Plus/Getty Images; p. 7 Kevin Dodge/The Image Bank/Getty Images; p. 9 Ronnie Kaufman/The Image Bank/Getty Images; p. 11 shironosov/iStock/Getty Images Plus/Getty Images; p. 13 Jamie Grill/The Image Bank/Getty Images; p. 15 Joe McBride/The Image Bank/Getty Images; p. 17 SDI Productions/E+/Getty Images; p. 19 Jordan Lye/Moment/Getty Images; p. 21 MoMo Productions/DigitalVision/Getty Images; p. 23 ER Productions Limited/DigitalVision/Getty Images.

CPSIA compliance information: Batch #CS22CSQ: For further information contact Cavendish Square Publishing LLC, New York, New York, at 1-877-980-4450.

Printed in the United States of America

CONTENTS

What Is Jealousy?

Have you ever felt jealous? Jealousy means you're **upset** that someone has something you don't. Jealousy is a **normal** feeling for people of all ages. It's OK to feel jealous sometimes.

You might feel jealous if someone gets something you want. Your brother might get a phone before you do. Your friend might get shoes that you want. It might not feel fair when others get things you want.

You might feel jealous if you think someone is more **special** than you. Maybe it's your sister's birthday. She's getting presents. People sing to her. You don't feel as special as your sister.

You might feel jealous at school. Maybe a teacher calls on someone else instead of you. Maybe someone else wins a race or gets a higher grade than you. This might make you upset.

You might feel jealous if someone you love spends time with someone else. You might feel jealous if your friend makes a new friend. You might feel jealous if your mom has a new baby.

Feeling Jealous

Jealousy can feel a lot like anger. Your face might feel hot. You might feel **tense**. Maybe you want to yell or say something mean. Maybe you want to take something from someone.

Jealousy can also feel like worry or sadness. You might worry someone loves you less. You might worry people won't like you without the right clothes. You might be sad about what you don't have. You might cry or **mope**.

Dealing with Jealousy

Jealousy can be a hard feeling to deal with. It's OK to feel jealous sometimes. You can learn how to deal with these feelings. First, try to **calm** down. Breathe in and out slowly.

Think about how you feel. Are you angry with the other person? Did they do something to hurt you? What do you really want? Talk to someone about what you want or how you feel.

We can't have everything we want. Maybe your friend got a dog. You can try to be happy for them. Ask to play! Sometimes it helps to make a list of what you do have. What are you thankful for?